LUCKY BUNNIES

Petal's Party

by Catherine Coe

Illustrated by Chie Boyd

■SCHOLASTIC

Published in the UK by Scholastic, 2022
Euston House, 24 Eversholt Street, London, NW1 1DB
Scholastic Ireland, 89E Lagan Road, Dublin Industrial Estate, Glasnevin, Dublin, D11 HP5F

SCHOLASTIC and associated logos are trademarks and/or registered trademarks of
Scholastic Inc.

First published in the US by Scholastic Inc, 2020

Text © Catherine Coe, 2020
Inside illustrations by Chie Boyd © Scholastic Inc, 2020
Cover illustration © Andrew Farley represented by Meiklejohn, 2022

The right of Catherine Coe, Chie Boyd and Andrew Farley to be identified
as the author and illustrators of this work has been asserted by them under the Copyright,
Designs and Patents Act 1988.

ISBN 978 1407 18865 2

A CIP catalogue record for this book is available from the British Library.

Printed by CPI Group (UK) Ltd, Croydon, CR0 4YY

Paper made fr   urces.

This is a work of f   roducts of
the author's imagi   le, living or

Contents

Bright Burrow

BASIL FOREST

MIRROR LAKE

RADISE BEACH

RADISH HIGH SCHOOL

CUCUMBER ROW

HAY ARENA

CARROT CENTRAL

STRAWBERRY FIELDS

For Leonie, who puts on the
BEST parties xxx

Not Any Rabbit Hole

This looks like a rabbit hole, right? It's small, round and muddy, with just enough space for a bunny to hop in, burrow around, sleep and eat.

But as you may have noticed, sometimes what seems to be on the outside is very different on the inside. And that's true nowhere more so than here.

For this isn't any rabbit hole. This one holds a special secret. A magical secret.

Inside this rabbit hole is the huge, amazing world of the Lucky Bunnies.

So watch your head, and come on in.

Welcome to the magical land of Bright Burrow...

ONE
Invitations

Petal couldn't stay still as she sat behind her log desk at school on Monday morning. Her fluffy pink tail twitched and her long, floppy ears flicked from side to side.

"Petal, do you need the bathroom?" Mr Nibble asked from his desk at the front of the classroom. As usual, the teacher was eating

something. Today, it was a parsnip almost the size of him.

"No, no!" Petal squeaked. "Not at all. I am absolutely fine!"

From her desk next to Petal, Diamond frowned. Petal didn't look fine. It wasn't that she looked unhappy. In fact, she was smiling. She just looked

as if she was bursting to do something! Diamond wondered what it might be.

She didn't have to wait long to find out. When the bell rang for playtime, Petal hopped from her desk as if there were a firework under her tail. She called to her friends to follow her out from their classroom, which was inside a large oak tree trunk.

"Diamond, Ruby, Star, Twinkle and Sky, come on!" Petal pulled on her friends' paws to drag them outside. The six bunnies scampered out into the dandelion field that surrounded Dandelion School. The school was made up of five classes – with each classroom inside the trunk of a different tree.

"Ta-da!" Petal said, and she held up five things

high above her pink head. As Petal was the tallest of the friends, the others couldn't quite see what they were.

"Ooh, is it a magic trick?" Sky asked. She flipped into the air to get a better look and saw there were five dock-leaf envelopes in Petal's paws.

Petal shook her head, making her gigantic floppy ears flap around her. "No, it's not a magic trick — they're invitations!"

Twinkle clapped his tiny mint-green paws together. "Invitations?" he squealed. "How furbulous! What are they for?"

Petal brought down her paws and passed the envelopes out to her friends. "You'll have to open them to find out!" she said.

Everyone began opening their envelopes.

Diamond did so carefully, putting a white claw under the flap to open it without tearing it. Star ripped into hers with her teeth, desperate to see what was inside.

"A Lucky Bunny burrow party!" Star said, reading the heading at the top of the invitation. Petal had decorated the barknote with flowers

and tiny leaves, and in the middle were the words:

Where: Petal's burrow
When: Saturday at noon
Don't forget: A party rat!

"Isn't it exciting?" Petal said. "We've never had a Lucky Bunny burrow party before!"

Twinkle jumped up and spun on the spot. "It's fantabulous!" he squeaked.

"Awesome!" Ruby added, nodding her glossy red head. "But what's a *party rat*?"

"Pardon?" Petal said. Ruby passed her the invitation, and Petal brought it right up to her eyes. "Oops-a-daisy! That should say party *hat*,

6

not party *rat*!" She giggled. "Sorry!"

"Phew," Sky chirped. "I didn't like the sound of a party rat!"

"Will there be room in your burrow, Petal?" Star asked. "What about all of your brothers?"

"That's absolutely the best part," Petal explained. "Luckily, they're all away on a school trip!" Petal had nine older brothers who went to Radish High School. Her burrow was normally so crowded there was no space to have her friends over.

"What did the party hat say to the bow tie?" Sky asked all of a sudden. Her friends shrugged.

"What?" said Petal.

"Don't tire yourself out!" Sky laughed. "Get it? Tie-re yourself out?"

Everyone giggled, except Star, who shook her golden head and rolled her eyes. "Where do you get your jokes from, Sky?"

Sky looked shocked and put a paw to her fluffy blue chest. "I don't get them from anywhere," she said. "I make them all up myself!"

Diamond twitched her white whiskers and said, "I thought it was funny, Sky. My dad takes ages tying up his tie for work, and it makes me tired just watching him."

"Hey, thanks, Diamond," Sky replied. She turned to Petal. "So what will we be doing at the burrow party, Petal? Have you got any ideas for games?"

Petal's smile almost reached her ears. "I have *so* many ideas!" she said. "I don't know where

to start! There's pin the tail on the bunny, and musical rabbits, and the lucky daisy game. And I thought we could have carrot crisps, and blueberry ice pops, and Five-Flower Fizz drinks—"

BRIIIIIING!

The bell rang for the end of playtime before Petal could finish. As they dashed back towards their classroom in the oak tree, Ruby scampered over to Petal. "It sounds like you totally need some lists to plan your burrow party," Ruby said, and her red curly whiskers twitched with excitement. "Can I help you?"

"Yes, please!" Petal put an arm

around Ruby. "Thank you. There's an awful lot to do, and I want it to be amazing!"

TWO
Basil Forest

"I can't walk home with you today," Star said as the six friends walked out of Dandelion School at the end of the day. "I've got to go to Basil Forest."

"Me too," squeaked Twinkle.

"Ooh, me three!" added Sky, and she did a forward flip with excitement.

"Me four!" Ruby said, holding up four fingers

on her paw. "How about you, Diamond and Petal? Can you come, too?"

"I can't today," Petal said. "Dad promised to take me to Cucumber Row to go shopping for party decorations."

"I've got my extra maths lesson," said Diamond, her voice quiet and shy. "But have fun!"

Diamond and Petal waved goodbye as they turned left out of the school gates. They hopped away towards Warren Street, the maze of burrows where the bunnies lived.

Twinkle, Sky, Star and Ruby turned right towards Sparkle River. Basil Forest was far past that – over on the other side of Bright Burrow – so far away they couldn't even see the trees of the forest in the distance.

They were about to hop over the silver stepping stones in Sparkle River when Sky gave a shout and pointed into the sky at something speeding through the air. "Ooh, that's lucky, we can catch the Clover Train to Basil Forest!" The Clover Train was a magical train made of giant four-leaf clover leaves that transported bunnies all around Bright Burrow. It didn't run on the ground but flew through the air, which meant it could go anywhere.

"Awesome," Ruby said. "We'll be so much quicker that way!"

The four bunnies waved to stop the Clover Train, and it zoomed down towards them until it hovered just above the ground.

"All aboard, all aboard!" called the conductor

from the front of the train. Star grinned — the conductor was her gran, Edna. She was the same size as Star, with the same large, pointy ears and golden fur, except Edna's was flecked with silver.

"Hello, Gran," said Star as she hopped on to the first four-leaf clover. It bounced a little as she jumped on, but Star knew she wouldn't fall off — it was impossible to do so. The Clover Train kept its travellers on board like magic, no matter how fast it flew.

Edna smiled a wrinkly smile as Ruby, Twinkle and Sky leaped on to the train behind Star. "Where would you like to go?" Star's gran asked.

"Basil Forest, please!" the four friends said together.

Edna tipped her green conductor's hat. "Basil

Forest it is! All right, bunnies. Mind your tails and get ready for departure!"

The leaves of the Clover Train shuddered under their feet for a moment, then zoomed off into the air. Sky squeaked as the wind whistled past her fluffy blue ears and the train climbed up into the sky. She never got tired of riding the Clover Train – from here she could see all across Bright Burrow, from Dandelion School to Basil Forest and everything in between. They sped over Sparkle River, where some bunnies were bathing in the water. Many of the older rabbits believed swimming in the river kept them young, so they spent a *lot* of time there. Sky just thought it made them wrinklier! There was Pineapple Square, the main meeting place in Bright Burrow, with its rabbit-shaped clock tower. Inside the tower was the Weather Rabbit – a mechanical silver rabbit in charge of changing the weather. It was a cloudy grey day today, and Sky crossed her paws, hoping that they'd be lucky and the Weather Rabbit wouldn't pop out to make it rain. And above them was the Luck Rainbow, seeming almost close enough to touch! The rainbow always shone over Bright Burrow, and if one of the colours was shining more brightly than the others, the bunnies believed it meant a certain type of luck was around that day.

The train zoomed over Paradise Beach, where bunnies were

digging all across the sand. With a bit of luck, a magical surprise could be found deep within the beach, which attracted lots of bunnies – young and old – to dig there.

"Get ready to land!" Edna called from the front of the train, and the four-leaf clover leaves began descending over Mirror Lake, with Basil Forest just on the other side. It landed with the tiniest of bumps on the edge of the forest.

Sky did a backflip off the train. "Thank you!" she chirruped to Edna.

"That was so awesome," said Ruby with a wave.

"Burrow-tastic!" added Twinkle.

"Can you take us back home later?" Star asked her gran.

Edna shrugged. "If you're lucky enough to

see me with an empty train, then yes, wave me down. Those are the rules!" The bunnies of Bright Burrow could only stop the train if no one was on it — but then they could ask it to go anywhere. It meant that Edna never had two days at work that were the same!

The four bunnies waved goodbye to Edna and began scampering into the forest. "I've got to find some parsley for my dad for our supper," Ruby said. Parents often sent their children to Basil Forest to collect herbs for cooking and healing. "How about everyone else?" Ruby asked her friends. "What do you have to get?"

"Parsley!" they all said at once.

"That's lucky! I guess we're all having parsley soup for supper then, hey!" Sky laughed.

Ruby pulled her list of the herbs that could be found in Basil Forest out of her school bag. She'd made a note of all of them, and exactly where they could be found. "The parsley patch is all the way over on the north side," Ruby said.

Star was looking over her shoulder. "Excellent list!" she told Ruby.

The bunnies darted north through the forest, and Twinkle breathed in deeply as he went. Incredible smells of basil, oregano, rosemary and thyme floated up his nose. The forest was one of his favourite places – the huge herbs growing everywhere made him feel as if he were in another world. But he didn't have time to daydream today – the tiny mint-green bunny was the smallest of his friends by far, and he had to run twice as fast to keep up with the others.

At last, they reached the parsley patch, where the gigantic bright green herbs towered over the bunnies' heads like trees. The friends chatted about Petal's burrow party as they picked out the ripest stems.

"Hey, the games Petal has planned sound great, don't you think?" Sky said. She leaped up and bit off a deep green piece of parsley and added it to her pile on the ground.

Star nodded and said, "I'm going to start practising musical rabbits right away." Her friends smiled. Star often took games a bit too seriously — but that did mean she usually won!

"Do you think she'll have karaoke?" Twinkle squeaked. "Singing is so furbulous, I could sing all night!" He flung out his paws and began to sing, *"How fluffy is that bunny in the burrow? As fluffy as fluffy can be..."*

Ruby's curly whiskers turned downwards. "I don't like singing so much," she said. "And it's not really a game, is it?"

"I didn't say it was a game, Ruby," Twinkle told her. "I just said that it's furbulous!"

"Well, not everyone thinks that!" Ruby replied. "Why do we have to always do what you want?"

Twinkle wriggled both of his pale green ears, feeling annoyed. "I didn't say that we did."

"But we do, loads," Ruby continued. She dropped her bunch of parsley and put her paws

on her red hips. "Yesterday we swam in Mirror Lake because you wanted to, and on Saturday we went to the nail bar because you needed yours trimmed."

"You didn't have to come," squeaked Twinkle, his voice even higher than usual. "You could have just stayed at home!"

"So you didn't want me to be there?" said Ruby. "Thanks a LOT!" And with that she scooped up her pile of parsley and stomped off across the forest.

"Did you have to say that?" Star said to Twinkle as Ruby hopped away, soon fading to a red dot in the distance.

Now it was Twinkle who put his paws on his hips. "Say what?" he said. "I didn't do anything

wrong. It was Ruby who shouted at me!" Twinkle stomped a tiny paw on the ground. "I'm going home!" he squeaked. "I'll see you at school tomorrow!" Before Star or Sky could say anything to stop him, Twinkle stuck the bunch of parsley he'd plucked into his mouth and ran off.

"Oh no," said Star. "School will be difficult if Twinkle and Ruby are arguing." She rubbed her velvety golden chin with a paw. "And what about Petal's party?"

Sky waved a paw in the air. "They'll be fine. It's ages until Saturday – there's no way they'll still be arguing by then. In fact, I bet you anything they'll have made up by the morning!"

THREE
Changing Places

Sky was wrong. Twinkle and Ruby hadn't made up the next morning. Not at all. When Sky and Diamond scampered into the classroom – they always walked to school together because they lived in next-door burrows – Ruby had swapped desks with their classmate Toppy so she wouldn't have to sit beside Twinkle.

"Why is Ruby sitting at Toppy's desk?" Diamond asked Sky.

Sky put a fluffy blue paw to her forehead. "Ooh no. They had an argument yesterday while we were picking parsley at Basil Forest," Sky explained. "I thought they would have made up by now!"

Mr Nibble began to take the register, chewing a stem of lemongrass at the side of his mouth as he spoke. "Diamond? Flo? Haybury? Jewel? Lopsy? Petal? Rainbow? Ruby? Sky? Star? Toppy? Twinkle? Twinkle...?"

Everyone replied yes to their name – apart from Twinkle. He was late – but that was normal for him. He was hardly ever on time for anything, not even school.

"Do you think Twinkle is so upset he's not coming today?" Star whispered to Sky.

Sky gulped. She hadn't thought of that. But the argument between Twinkle and Ruby hadn't been that bad. Sky couldn't even remember what it was about, really.

Just then a blur of mint-green fur shot into the classroom. "Sorry I'm late, Mr Nibble!" Twinkle squeaked.

Sky let out a long sigh of relief.

Twinkle hopped to his log desk and settled himself down. Then he turned to the left – where Ruby normally sat – and frowned.

Ooh no, he's seen that Ruby's changed places! thought Sky.

Twinkle looked around the classroom,

squinting and twitching his tiny nose. When he spotted Ruby, all the way over on the other side of the tree-trunk classroom, he scowled and shook his head.

"Uh-oh," Star said under her breath.

Petal was twisting her head, confused. "What's going on?" Petal whispered to Star.

"They had a small ... disagreement yesterday," Star said.

"Oh dear! That's terrible." Petal put her pink head in her paws. She hated it when her friends argued.

"But I'm super sure they'll make up today!" Sky chirruped, not very quietly.

Mr Nibble raised his black-and-white head and took the stem of lemongrass from his mouth. "What are you chattering about back there?" he asked with a frown.

"Nothing, Mr Nibble!" Star said quickly.

"Hmm, it didn't sound like nothing," their teacher replied. "Anyway, there's no time for chatting this morning – take out your reading books, please. We're going to continue where we left off yesterday with *The Tale of Peter Rabbit*, page eight. Twinkle, can you read the first page, please?"

Twinkle began reading aloud in his squeaky, high voice. "'Mr McGregor was quite sure that Peter was somewhere in the toolshed, perhaps hidden underneath a flowerpot. He began to turn them over carefully, looking under each.'" Twinkle did the actions as he read, pretending to turn over imaginary flowerpots. It looked as if he was enjoying himself *a lot*.

The students took turns reading a page aloud. Some of the bunnies enjoyed it more than others. Diamond didn't like reading out loud at all – she felt shy with everyone listening to her, and her quiet voice came out in barely a whisper. But

Mr Nibble clapped when she'd finished. "That was your best reading yet, Diamond," he said. "Well done."

Diamond felt her white cheeks blush as Sky started to read the next page. She put on funny

voices for the different characters, which made her classmates laugh.

"Thank you, Sky. That was really... entertaining," said Mr Nibble, just as the bell rang for playtime.

As Oak Class skipped out of the tree trunk to the dandelion field, Star had almost forgotten about Ruby and Twinkle's argument. Then she saw that the two bunnies were glaring at each other while the others munched on dandelion flowers.

"Whatever is wrong?" asked Petal, looking between the two bunnies. "What happened yesterday? Star said you had a disagreement?"

Neither of them replied, so Sky said, "There *was* a bit of an argument yesterday. But it's nothing to worry about – right, Ruby? Twinkle?"

Still the two bunnies didn't say anything.

Petal flapped her ears around in worry and turned to Sky and Star. "What was their argument about?"

"You know, I'm not really sure. . . " Sky began.

"It was about the party," Star explained. She always remembered *everything*. It was usually a

good thing, but not always. Sometimes things were better forgotten. "Twinkle wants to do karaoke, and Ruby doesn't."

"It's not that I don't want to do karaoke!" Ruby butted in, twitching her curly whiskers furiously. "It's just that we *always* do what Twinkle wants."

"That's not true!" squealed Twinkle.

"Hey!" Sky jumped up and waved her fluffy arms about between her friends to stop them from fighting again.

Petal took a very long and very deep breath. Then she flapped one long ear around Twinkle and one around Ruby. "Please, please, please don't argue," she said. "Especially about the party. It's supposed to be for us to have fun, not to fight.

Why don't you apologize to each other, and you can both forget it ever happened?"

"But Twinkle started it," said Ruby.

"What?" Twinkle squeaked. He was so upset, his little ears were shaking. "No, I certainly did not!"

"Please!" Petal begged them again. "Please say you're sorry."

Twinkle shrugged away from Petal's ear-hug. "Why should I?" he said.

"And why should I?" Ruby added, ducking out of Petal's grip, too. "You can't make us!"

And they each ran off to opposite sides of the dandelion field.

Petal twitched her nose, gave a sniff and burst into tears. Diamond hopped over and took her

paw. "Please don't cry, Petal."

"It'll be OK," Sky added, trying to sound just as chirpy as usual, although she didn't feel it.

"Will it really be all right?" said Petal as she blinked away tears. "I don't know that it will. They've never, ever argued like this before. And it's all my party's fault! What if they haven't made up by Saturday?"

Sky, Diamond and Star didn't know what to say to that, so they didn't say anything at all. They munched on their dandelion flowers in silence as Petal put her head in her paws.

FOUR
Pawfect Presents

At lunch time on Wednesday, Star pulled Sky, Petal and Diamond over to one corner of the field. Twinkle had stayed behind in their classroom, to work on his paw-painting for art. Ruby had gone home for lunch, saying that she needed to help her mum write her shopping lists. The two bunnies still hadn't made up since their argument.

"We have to do something!" said Star as she stomped a hind foot. She was fed up with her two friends not speaking and determined to do something about it.

Petal wrung her paws together. "But what?" she said. "They won't say they're sorry. They won't even look at each other! So how will we be lucky enough to persuade them to make up?"

"Maybe they don't have to look at each other," Diamond said thoughtfully.

"Huh?" Sky chirruped. "What do you mean?"

"The last time my parents had an argument,

my dad gave my mum a present to say he was sorry," Diamond explained.

"But I don't think we'll be able to persuade Ruby and Twinkle to buy each other presents," Star said.

"Nope," Sky agreed. "But we don't need to. We could get presents for them!"

Petal looked up, suddenly feeling hopeful. "And everyone likes presents!" she said.

Star put a paw to her chin and talked it through. "So we buy presents for Ruby and Twinkle and give them to each other, pretending they're from the other one...Yes, that could work. Great thinking, Diamond!"

As soon as the bell rang after school, Star, Petal, Diamond and Sky hopped out of the classroom. Petal stuck her front paws in her ears as she ran – the loud school bell always made her brain jangle.

Once they'd left the school gates, Star looked up into the sky, hoping they'd be lucky enough to catch the Clover Train, but she couldn't see the four-leaf clover leaves anywhere. They'd have to hop to Cucumber Row themselves. But it wasn't too far – just on the other side of Sparkle River.

The four friends soon reached the shiny green cobbles of Cucumber Row, the main shopping street in Bright Burrow. It was full of bunnies of every shape, size and colour doing their shopping. Some of the older bunnies were hopping along slowly, chatting as they went.

Some bunnies carried baskets of vegetables, and some wore little rucksacks with their shopping poking out.

"There are so very many shops to choose from!" Petal said as she looked up and down the street. "Where should we start?"

"Mrs Whiskers's Pawfect Presents," said Star firmly. "It's the best place for gifts."

Mrs Whiskers's shop was at the other end of Cucumber Row, so they began scampering towards it.

"Ooh, look," Sky chirruped as they passed the tail-dresser, Fur Real. Sparkly hair clips hung across the window like bunting. "Can we go in?"

"No!" said Star. "We've got to get the presents first."

Petal gave Star a look, and Star realized how bossy she'd sounded.

"Sorry, Sky," Star said. "I just really want Twinkle and Ruby to make up. With any luck, there'll be time to go to Fur Real later."

"Ooh, OK!" Sky smiled, and the friends continued hopping down the street.

They passed Skip and Clip, the nail bar, and Bright Burrow Tails, the bookshop. Finally, they arrived outside Pawfect Presents. Today, the window was filled with balls of every kind – footballs, basketballs, baseballs and golf balls. Even juggling balls and beach balls!

Petal stepped in first. As she pushed the door open, it was like entering an enchanted cave. The shop was a maze of nooks and crannies and filled with lanterns that lit up every corner. The shelves and tables were covered in every gift imaginable – toys, games, sweets, soaps, candles and jewellery. The air smelled as sweet as honey, and some soft guitar music played gently in the background.

"I love this shop," said Diamond softly as she stepped in behind Petal.

A rummaging sound came from behind the counter at the very back, and a chestnut-brown head popped up above it. "Hello, my dears!" said Mrs Whiskers. She waved, making the many bead necklaces around her neck jingle like bells. "What can I do for you today?"

"We're looking for two extra-special presents," Petal told the shopkeeper. "Can you help us at all?"

Mrs Whiskers stepped out from behind the wooden counter. "You're in luck! How about a willow weave pencil case? They're new in today!" She held up one of the pencil cases that had

been made with hundreds of coloured willow leaves all woven together.

Sky hopped closer to get a better look. "Hmm ... sure, they're cute. What do you think, Star?"

Star shook her head. "They're nice, but not quite right. And each present has to be perfect," Star added. "To give it the best chance of working."

"Don't you mean 'pawfect'?" Sky chirped. "You know, because this is Pawfect Presents?"

Star rolled her eyes at Sky's joke.

"Oh, look at these gorgeous soaps," Petal said. She held up a rabbit-shaped soap in a pink paw, and then squealed as it slipped from her fingers. "Oops-a-daisy!"

Mrs Whiskers darted over and caught the soap in her fluffy brown tail before it hit the floor.

"Hey, you're fast, Mrs Whiskers!" Sky said, impressed.

The shopkeeper winked. "Customers drop things a lot. I have to keep on my toes!"

Star started looking around the rest of the shop and noticed Diamond was bent over a shelf in the corner. "Did you find something?" Star asked.

Diamond turned and nodded. "Ruby might like this silver-birch notepad," she said, and picked up a notepad made of silvery bark paper. "Because she likes to write a lot of lists, doesn't she?"

Star did a little jump. "It's perfect!" she said. "I mean, *pawfect!*" she added before Sky could correct her.

The others, including Mrs Whiskers, giggled.

"All right, so now we need something wonderful for Twinkle," Petal said. She hopped over to the sweets. "He likes beetroot fudge, doesn't he?" This time she decided not to pick anything up, just in case she dropped it again.

"Ooh, I think so!" said Sky.

"But he got lots of fudge for his birthday," Star said, remembering that Twinkle had brought beetroot fudge in his lunch box to school for weeks afterwards. He'd shared it with his friends every day, which Star thought had been very generous, considering it was his favourite.

Diamond spun around and at the same time made a strange jingling sound, as if she were wearing bells on her  ankles. Petal looked over and squinted. With her bad eyesight, she couldn't quite see what was in Diamond's paws.

"A tambourine!" Mrs Whiskers said. "The pawfect present for anyone who likes music and singing."

Star did a hop of happiness. "That describes Twinkle exactly! We'll take it!"

"Can I try it out, Diamond?" Sky asked. Diamond passed the instrument to Sky, and she began shaking it around. The next moment, Sky had

slipped it over her head and was spinning it around her waist like a hula-hoop, dancing about as it jingled. The other bunnies clapped and laughed – sometimes Sky really was hilarious.

When Sky had finished her dance, she gave Mrs Whiskers the tambourine. The shopkeeper wrapped both presents up in cream cotton paper and tied them with giant red bows.

They look so pretty! thought Diamond.

"Now it's time to deliver them!" Star declared.

"Thank you for coming, my dears. I hope your friends like their presents," Mrs Whiskers said as they left the shop.

So do I, thought Petal. *Otherwise I don't know what we'll do!*

FIVE
The Music Lesson

"Did you deliver Ruby's present safely?" Star whispered to Sky and Diamond the next morning as they arrived at school.

"Yep!" Sky whispered back. "And guess what? She loved it!"

"Luckily, Twinkle loved his present, too," Star said. She and Petal had taken the tambourine

to Twinkle last night, while Sky and Diamond had delivered Ruby's present. "Look!" Star added, and pointed a golden paw to the door of the hollow tree trunk.

Twinkle was running into the classroom – not late for once – with the tambourine tucked under his arm. He sat down at his desk and smiled when he saw Ruby had moved back to her usual desk beside his.

Ruby took out her new notepad from her school bag and laid it carefully on her log desk. She turned to Twinkle. "Thank you," she said, and held up the notepad. "It's totally awesome."

"Pardon?" said Twinkle, confused. He'd never seen the notepad before.

At that moment, Mr Nibble started taking the

register – with a mouthful of daisies – so Ruby couldn't answer Twinkle. Petal looked over at Ruby and Twinkle, and her heart jittered with worry. She realized then that there was a huge problem with their plan – unless they were really lucky, Ruby and Twinkle would each find out that the other one hadn't sent the present!

"We'll start with music today," Mr Nibble said, a few daisy petals flying out of his mouth as he spoke. "We're going to learn a new song."

Petal relaxed a bit – hopefully that would mean there'd be no time for Twinkle and Ruby to talk.

"Everyone, grab a pair of bongos." Mr Nibble pointed at the barkboard behind him, where he'd written the words to the song.

Twinkle stuck up his paw, but he was so tiny that Mr Nibble didn't see it. Twinkle jumped up and down. "Mr Nibble!" he squeaked.

Their teacher looked down at Twinkle. "Yes?" he said.

"Can I play my tambourine instead?" Twinkle asked. He held up the instrument, and the bells on it tinkled softly.

Mr Nibble came over to admire the tambourine. "I don't see why not, Twinkle. It's lovely. Where did you get it from?"

Twinkle grinned and darted a look over at Ruby. "It was a present, Mr Nibble. From Ruby."

"Oh, how nice," Mr Nibble said, but Twinkle wasn't really listening any more. He was wondering why Ruby had the biggest frown on her face and her normally curly whiskers were suddenly sticking out straight.

Mr Nibble hopped back to the front of the room and pointed to the first line of the song.

"What are you talking about?" Ruby whispered to Twinkle. "I totally didn't get you that. You got me this!" And she held up the pretty silvery notepad.

"NO," Twinkle squeaked. "*You* got me *this!*" He heard Petal groan, and he turned to her. Petal's pink face had gone the colour of beetroot fudge. She flapped both her ears across her eyes.

That was when Twinkle realized what had happened. Star and Petal had brought him the present from Ruby last night — but it wasn't really from Ruby. They'd just done it to try to get them to make up. And they'd done the same thing with Ruby and the notepad!

Twinkle dropped the tambourine, and it crashed to the floor. "Actually,

Mr Nibble, I don't want to play the tambourine after all." He ran to the music cupboard to get a set of bongos.

Mr Nibble began to teach the class the song, and Twinkle bashed the bongo drums as hard as he could. He should have known the tambourine wasn't a present from Ruby. She was too stubborn for that!

Petal couldn't concentrate on learning the song. All she could think about was Twinkle and Ruby, and how angry they both looked as they slapped their paws against their bongos. The banging sounds rattled in Petal's ears until she had the biggest headache.

The lesson seemed to go on for ever, but at last the bell rang for playtime. The *briiinging* sound made her head hurt even worse, but at least the drumming noises had stopped.

Outside, Ruby and Twinkle darted away to opposite sides of the field before their friends could stop them.

"Oh dear. This is dreadful," said Petal, her voice high with worry. "Whatever can we do?"

Star glanced over at Twinkle. "I'll go and speak to him," she said. "I'll see if I can calm him down. Sky, will you come with me? Twinkle normally listens to you."

"Yep, sure thing," Sky chirruped. The two bunnies scampered over to where Twinkle sat among the dandelions. He was pulling up the flowers as if they were his worst enemies.

"Let's go and talk to Ruby," Diamond suggested to Petal, and the two friends quickly hopped over to the other side of the field.

As they got closer, Diamond saw that Ruby was still holding the silver-birch notepad. She was staring at it, a sad look on her face.

Ruby heard the pawsteps of Diamond and Petal and looked up.

"Why did you totally lie about the presents?" Ruby asked.

"I'm so very sorry!" Petal said. "We were just trying to help you and Twinkle make up."

"We didn't mean to make things worse," added Diamond. "We only fibbed so that we could make things *better*."

Ruby sniffed. "You should know that you

should never lie to friends. Even if it is for a good reason."

"It was a terrible mistake," said Petal. "But will you _please_ make up with Twinkle?"

Ruby sniffed again. "Totally — if he says sorry."

Petal's hopes rose and fell in one go. It didn't

seem as if Twinkle was ready to apologize. What would they do if he didn't?

"We'll go and ask him," Diamond told Ruby. "Stay there."

Diamond and Petal dashed over to the tiny figure of Twinkle, surrounded by the fluffy blue Sky and the golden shiny Star.

"Are you sure you can't say you're sorry?" Sky was asking Twinkle.

"No!" Twinkle squeaked. "I don't see why I should apologize first!"

So that's it then, thought Petal. She hung her head and blinked as she tried to stop her tears from falling. Their plan had been a disaster, and now it looked as if it might ruin their friendships for ever. She was starting to think she should never have invited everyone to a Lucky Bunny burrow party. So far it hadn't been very lucky at all!

SIX
A New Plan

Friday wasn't any better than Thursday. Ruby had swapped desks with Toppy again, and Twinkle spent the whole of playtime and lunch time in the classroom working on his art project.

"I think I should cancel the party," Petal said sadly as she, Sky, Star, Diamond and Ruby sat in the

dandelion field eating their lunches. Petal's cress sandwiches sat untouched in her lunch box. She didn't feel hungry *at all*.

"Nooo, you can't do that!" Sky said. "It's your first Lucky Bunny burrow party!"

Petal flicked her long ears over her shoulders. "But it won't feel very lucky without Ruby and Twinkle."

Star stared at Ruby. "Just come, will you, Ruby?"

Ruby sighed and her curly whiskers drooped. "I already told you, I'm not going if Twinkle's going to be there," she said.

Petal thought hard, trying to come up with a way to fix this. If Twinkle came to the party, Ruby wouldn't come. And if Ruby came, Twinkle wouldn't. But Petal couldn't choose between her two friends!

The bell rang for afternoon lessons, and the five bunnies walked back slowly to the oak tree, set in the middle of the group of tree-trunk classrooms.

As they hopped through the field, Diamond tapped Petal on the arm. "I'm not sure if I can come either," Diamond said, her white ears turning down as she spoke. "My mum and dad want me to help with a bake sale they're having."

"But didn't you tell them my party is on Saturday?" Petal squeaked. Her heart plunged with disappointment all over again.

"Yes," Diamond said. Her voice was so quiet Petal could hardly hear it over the rustle of the wind blowing the leaves in the trees. "But they still want me to help. . ."

Petal wondered whether Diamond's parents were really having a bake sale or whether it was an excuse Diamond made up because she was shy. Maybe she was worried about playing the games with everyone and being embarrassed.

Petal decided not to push her friend. That wouldn't help persuade her. Instead Petal told Diamond, "I very much hope you can come. You

don't have to join in with the games if you don't want to."

Diamond nodded and gave Petal a little smile. "Thanks, Petal. I'll try my best. I promise."

As they entered the classroom, Star tugged on Sky's fluffy blue tail to stop her from going inside. "Ooh, ouch!" Sky squealed. "What did you do that for?"

"I'm sorry," Star apologized. She was hopping from paw to paw just outside the tree trunk. "But I need to speak to you. Petal's party is tomorrow. We have to do something before then!"

Sky's fuzzy ears shot upwards, and she wiggled her very fluffy eyebrows. "You're right. It's up to us. We're Lucky Bunnies, and we can fix this!" Sky chirped. She did a backflip into the classroom and landed at her desk.

As Star followed her, she thought about how much she loved that Sky was always so positive. This time, more than any other, Star hoped that Sky was right.

On Saturday morning, after a breakfast of strawberry porridge, Ruby scampered towards Pineapple Square. Star and Sky had arranged to meet her there to play games on the chequered pavement. Sometimes the friends played Snakes and Ladders there together. Sometimes hopscotch. Sometimes they made up completely new games to play.

The square was empty when Ruby arrived. A moment later, the Weather Rabbit popped out of his tower. *Please don't make it rain,* Ruby thought. It was already so windy that Ruby's curly whiskers were getting blown everywhere. The Weather Rabbit opened his silver mechanical mouth and said:

"Wind, wind, go away. Be calm and bring out the sunshine to play!"

Ruby grinned up at the clock tower. "That's lucky. Thank you!" she said to the rabbit, as if he could hear her. She watched as he shuffled back inside the tower, wondering just how he worked, and how exactly he could change the weather in an instant.

As Ruby looked down again, a ball of mint-green fur darted in front of her. Ruby groaned. She'd recognize that shape anywhere. What was Twinkle doing here?

Before she could ask him, the Clover Train came out of nowhere, whizzing down from above, and coming to a halt beside the two bunnies.

"All aboard!" Edna called. "Both of you!"

Ruby twitched her red nose. "But I didn't call the train."

"Nor did I!" Twinkle said.

Edna hopped from the train and jumped behind the two bunnies to usher them on to the four-leaf clovers. "I know," she told them. "But lucky for you, Star and Sky did. You two are getting on this train, and you're not getting off until you've worked out your differences."

Edna hopped on behind them, and the Clover Train swooped off into the air, leaving Twinkle and Ruby stuck on it. Its magical power to keep bunnies safely on meant they couldn't jump off now even if they dared!

Ruby shook her head, realizing that Star and Sky had tricked her — and Twinkle, too. They weren't ever going to meet her at Pineapple Square. They had planned this all — for Ruby and Twinkle to be stuck on the train together.

"What are you doing here, Ruby?" Twinkle squeaked as the train sped high over Bright Burrow. "Where are Sky and Star?"

"I don't want to be here!" Ruby replied. "Don't you see? It was a trick — they were never really going to meet you here."

Twinkle gave a high growl. "A trick? Are you calling me stupid?" he asked. "How rude!"

"No, I didn't say you're stupid," Ruby called back. "And I'm totally not rude — you are!" She hopped to the very rear of the train, as far away from Twinkle as she could possibly get.

At the front of the Clover Train, Edna glanced over her shoulder and sighed. She'd wanted to help her granddaughter and her friends, but it looked like it might be a very long train ride...

SEVEN
Stuffed

A little while later, Star and Sky met at Pineapple Square.

Star pointed into the sky above Hay Arena, the stadium where many of the events and festivals in Bright Burrow were held. "There's the Clover Train," Star said. She could see the leaf carriages in the distance, but it was too far away to make out any bunnies aboard it. "With any luck, we won't have to wait too long before Gran brings them back," Star added. "I wanted to do some bouncing practice before Petal's party today." Star bounced every day without fail, and it paid off – she had been picked to take part in the annual Bounce-a-Lot festival every single year.

Sky did a cartwheel across the chequered pavement of the square. "I'm sure they'll make up!" she chirruped. "Now that they *have* to talk to each other, they've got to make up."

The two friends sat down to wait in front of the line of pineapple plants that edged the square.

Star looked behind her at a large ripe pineapple, bright yellow and juicy. "Shall we share a pineapple while we wait?" she asked.

Sky wriggled her little blue nose. "Ooh yep, sure thing!"

The gigantic fruit was almost as big as Sky. They munched and munched and munched, each bite flooding their mouths with the pineapple's sweet, sharp flavour.

"They'll definitely be back by the time we finish this!" Sky said, swallowing yet another mouthful. They'd been eating for ages now, but the pineapple didn't seem to be getting much smaller!

Both bunnies were feeling extremely full, but they kept going until they finally took their last

bite each and only the spiky green stalk at the top was left. The bunnies buried it back in its old spot – where a brand-new, delicious pineapple would soon grow again – and looked up. But the Clover Train was still far away in the distance.

Star began pacing up and down Pineapple Square. "I really thought this would work!" she said. "How much longer will they be? I'll never have time for bouncing practice now. Perhaps they'll never make up!"

"Hey, don't give up yet," Sky told her. She looked around for something else to do while they waited. When she didn't see anything helpful, a different idea popped into her head. "We can tell some jokes!" Sky chirruped.

Star twitched her golden nose and stopped

pacing. She plonked herself down next to Sky again. "All right, then. You go first."

"Sure!" Sky thought quickly and remembered a joke she'd told her mum and dad just that morning. "How can you tell when a dandelion is angry?" she asked Star.

Star frowned as she tried to think of the answer. "Hmmm...An angry dandelion...It doesn't make sense! Dandelions are just plants."

"It's a *joke*," Sky said. "Don't think about them being plants, think about them being angry!"

"I knows," said a strange voice behind them. "Dandelions shout when they're angry!"

Both Sky and Star hopped up and spun around in one fast movement. A black-and-white ferret stood grinning on the other side of the

line of pineapples. It was Hiss — a ferret the friends knew all too well. He liked to sneak into Bright Burrow and annoy the bunnies.

"I thought I smelled something awful," Star said, and she waved a paw in front of her nose.

"Hey, Hiss, what are you doing here?" Sky said. "You're not supposed to come into the burrow."

"Wells, I did, didn't I?" Hiss stood up on his hind legs to make himself seem bigger than the bunnies – he was even taller than Petal when he stood up like that. "Anyways, was I right?" he said. "About the joke?"

Sky wasn't scared of Hiss, even when he tried to make the bunnies frightened like this. He was too stupid to be truly scary. "Nope – you're wrong!" Sky said with great pleasure. "Now leave us alone!"

"Why should I?" said Hiss. "I likes being here." He scurried around and sat himself down on Pineapple Square – right in front of Sky and Star. "Now I'll tell a joke. What d'you call a squished—"

But Hiss didn't finish, because the Weather Rabbit popped out of the clock tower all of a sudden and yelled, "It's raining rain in Bright

Burrow, it's raining rain!" As the silver bunny spoke, fat droplets of rain began pouring down from the sky.

"Urgh, I HATES rain!" moaned Hiss. He shot up and darted away quicker than you could say "annoying ferret".

Star and Sky grinned. "That was lucky," chirped Sky.

"Thanks, Weather Rabbit," Star said to the silver figure, even though she was pretty sure he was a machine and couldn't hear her.

As the rain kept pouring, the droplets slid off Star's glossy short fur like oil, but Sky wasn't so lucky. She was trying to use her fluffy ears to protect the rest of her fur from the rain, but it didn't really work. In seconds, Sky looked as soggy as a sandwich that had been dunked in Mirror Lake.

"I think we should go home," Star suggested. "You're soaking, Sky. You'll need to dry off for Petal's party."

The party! With all the waiting, Sky had almost forgotten it, and it was only now that she saw what the time was on the large black-and-white face of the clock tower. She squealed and said, "There's no way we can go home first. It's nearly noon!"

Star followed Sky's gaze to the hands of the clock. The big hand was pointing exactly left, and the little hand was almost at the top. They'd been so busy waiting for their friends to make

up that they'd forgotten about keeping track of the time.

"What about Ruby and Twinkle?" Star asked.

Sky and Star looked upwards. The Clover Train still circled around, high in the air. Even though it was raining, there was no sign the train would be coming down any time soon.

"I really thought they would have made up by now," Sky said, her soaking blue ears dripping like a tap with the rain.

"We can't wait any longer." Star sighed.

Sky nodded, sending water droplets everywhere. "I know. And if we don't hurry up, we'll miss Petal's party, too. Let's go!"

They spun around and began hopping back towards Warren Street, their paws splashing in the puddles that now covered Bright Burrow. As they left Pineapple Square, they heard the Weather Rabbit behind them shout, "Rain, rain, go away!" and the rain stopped as suddenly as it had started.

"Excellent!" Star said with a flick of her ears. "With any luck, our fur will dry by the time we get to Petal's burrow."

The two bunnies hopped and skipped as fast as they could, and didn't even talk so they could focus on running. But as they leaped across the stepping stones dotted in Sparkle River, Star burst out with a "Roar!"

Sky stumbled in shock and almost slipped off a stone. "Huh?" she said.

"Your joke," Star explained. "The answer is roars!"

Sky made her final hop to the safety of the bank and clapped her paws together. "Right!" she chirped. "Because it's a dandeLION!"

Sky high-pawed Star as she jumped on to the bank beside her, and they sprinted all the way to Petal's burrow at the centre of Warren Street. They skidded to a stop at Petal's door, and Star pressed the heart-shaped doorbell with a paw.

DING-DONG, DING-DONG! They heard the chimes ring inside Petal's burrow. A second later, they could hear the heavy pads of Petal's paws as she rushed to the door.

"Hello!" she said brightly as she swung the door open. Behind it, Petal was wearing a beautiful pink ribbon around each ear, a stripy party hat and her tail had been styled into a pretty bow shape.

Star gulped. *We look dreadful*, she thought. *Not dressed for a party. We don't even have party hats!*

"It's such bad luck that the Weather Rabbit made it rain right when we were hopping to your burrow," Sky said. It wasn't quite the truth, of

course, but she didn't think now was the right time to explain what they'd been doing. Sky's blue fur had dried, but it had grown extra fluffy, and she could hardly see past her eyebrows.

Petal didn't seem to hear – she was looking over their heads instead. "Is it just the two of you?" she asked.

Star gulped and said, "I'm afraid so. I'm sorry." She thought of Twinkle and Ruby, *still* on the Clover Train.

"Oh," Petal said, and her mouth turned down. Then she clapped her paws together and smiled again. "Never mind. Three is still enough for a party. I hope you're hungry!"

Sky thought back to the gigantic pineapple she and Star had eaten earlier.

She wasn't hungry at all — but she couldn't tell Petal that. "I'm starving!" Sky fibbed, and Petal's smile grew wider.

Petal beckoned them into the burrow dining room where a log table had been piled high with all sorts of party treats. There were carrot crisps and kale cupcakes and parsnip pretzels and spinach sandwiches. A giant cake stand with four tiers held all sorts of desserts, including pear pies and mango muffins and banana buttons. There were even kiwi ice pops and rhubarb crumble ice cream. A huge jug of Five-Flower Fizz drink stood at one end of the table, surrounded by chestnut cups decorated with little rabbit umbrellas. Petal passed Sky and Star a dock-leaf plate each, but didn't take one for herself. "Dig in!" she said.

"Aren't you eating anything?" Star asked.

"Oh dear, no, I couldn't possibly eat any more," Petal said. "I tried everything as I was making it, and I'm absolutely stuffed!"

Star and Sky looked at each other, their eyes wide. "OK, then we'd better get started!" Sky chirruped. She began loading her dock-leaf with all the different treats.

After eating two platefuls of food, Star thought she might burst.

"Would you like some more?" Petal asked, heaving up the cake stand and holding it out to her two friends.

Star wiped her whiskers with a rose-petal napkin. "Maybe later," she said as politely as she

could. "It was all delicious, but shouldn't we play a game now?"

Petal's smile vanished again. "We can't! All the games I've prepared need at least four players," she explained.

Sky, who also couldn't eat another thing, said, "Sure you've prepared them for four, but we could try them with three, couldn't we?"

Petal nodded slowly, her long ears flopping forward. "I suppose—"

DING-DONG, DING-DONG! Petal was cut off by the doorbell. She hopped up, her black eyes sparkling. "Coming!" she called, and raced out of the dining room.

With all their fingers on all their paws crossed for luck, Star and Sky scampered behind her.

EIGHT
The Burrow Party

"Diamond!" Petal said when she opened the door. She flapped her ears around her friend in a hug. "You came after all!"

"Flippety-flop!" Star whispered to Sky. "I thought it was Ruby and Twinkle."

Sky nodded. "Me too," she whispered back.

"But hey, four is better than three, and it sure is nice to see Diamond!"

Diamond smiled shyly as Petal let her go from her ear-hug. "We sold the cakes at the bake sale really fast, so my parents let me come," Diamond explained in her quiet voice. "And I bought the last one — for you!" Diamond held out a heart-shaped cake covered in pink icing and scattered with tiny silver stars.

Petal put her paws to her face. "It's beautiful!" she declared. "Let's have a piece now, shall we?"

Sky groaned, louder than she'd meant to,

and everyone turned to her. The cake looked delicious, but there was no way Sky could eat even a bite.

"What's the matter?" Petal asked Sky, and her smile slipped away again.

"I'm sorry, Petal and Diamond," Sky said, "but I can't eat any of that cake right now."

Star patted Sky's paw. "Sky's right. We've eaten an enormous amount already."

With a sniff, Petal burst out crying. Her friends crowded around her as tears as big as raindrops dripped from her shiny black nose.

"Hey, Petal, please don't cry," Sky said. "We'll eat the cake somehow."

"I'm sorry — I shouldn't have brought it," Diamond said.

"No, no, it's not the cake that's made me upset," Petal snivelled. She wiped her eyes with one of her long, droopy ears. "I so miss all six of us being together. I mean, it's wonderful that the three of you are here, but the party just isn't the same without Ruby and Twinkle, too. I don't think they'll ever make up!"

Star didn't know what to say to that. Deep down, she agreed with Petal. It seemed as if Ruby and Twinkle would never be friends again.

"Hey, come on," Sky chirruped, trying to make the best of things. "Now that Diamond is here, we have four bunnies to play the games. We can still have fun. And we'll be able to eat the cake later!"

Petal nodded, sniffed, and said, "All right."

But she doesn't really sound all right, Diamond thought.

Petal hopped to the door to shut it. But luckily, just as she started to push it, she spotted something in the distance. She blinked and rubbed her eyes with an ear once more.

She could see two shapes scampering along the path and heading right for her burrow. Petal's poor eyesight meant she couldn't make out exactly who they were – not even what colour they were – but could it be...?

"Ruby! Twinkle!" Petal's friends yelled from behind her, and now Petal could see the bunnies more clearly – a medium-sized red bunny and a tiny mint-green one.

Petal's heart did a somersault, and she ran out to meet them. She wrapped each one in a giant ear-hug and danced them around in a circle while Ruby and Twinkle giggled.

"You made up!" Petal said as she finally let the two bunnies go and ushered them inside her burrow. "What happened?"

Sky and Star were waiting for the answer just as much as Petal. What *had* happened on the Clover Train?

Ruby and Twinkle glanced at each other. "It's a verrrrry long story," squeaked Twinkle.

"And, to be totally honest, I'm really thirsty," Ruby said.

"And sooo hungry," added Twinkle.

Petal beamed from one long, floppy ear to the other. "You're in luck!" She beckoned them through to the dining room and piled two plates high with food for Ruby and Twinkle while Star poured them two chestnut cups of Five-Flower Fizz drink. Then the six friends settled down on the soft velveteen sofa, and Ruby and Twinkle began their story.

"I was so angry at Twinkle, I thought we'd never make up," Ruby said. "And when Sky and Star fixed it so that we'd be on the Clover Train together by ourselves, we just started arguing again."

Twinkle swallowed a mouthful of kale cupcake and added, "And we sat at opposite ends of the train as we rode round and round Bright Burrow." As Twinkle spoke, Ruby munched on some parsnip pretzels. "Your gran tried to persuade us to make up, Star, but we wouldn't even speak to each other."

Twinkle took a slurp of his Five-Flower Fizz drink, and Ruby picked up the story. "Edna even started spinning the train in small circles, trying to make us dizzy. But that didn't work!"

"So what did?" asked Sky, sitting forward and putting her fluffy paws on her lap.

"The Clover Train took us over Warren Street," Twinkle squeaked. "I don't know whether Edna did it on purpose or whether it was luck, but the train was really low, so we could see everyone clearly."

Ruby chewed her lip. "And we saw you, Petal, at your door when Star and Sky arrived. You looked so sad."

"It made me cry!" Twinkle squeaked.

"Me too," Ruby added. "And it made our argument seem so totally stupid."

"I'm sorry!" Petal said, feeling dreadful. Ruby never cried!

"No, *we're* sorry!" Twinkle and Ruby said at

the same time. They hopped up and wrapped their arms around Petal. Sky, Star and Diamond leaped from the sofa and joined in the group hug.

"Can you forgive us?" Twinkle squeaked from the middle of the bunny hug.

Petal answered by bursting into tears.

"Please don't cry!" Ruby said.

Petal shook her head as more tears sprang to her eyes, and she used an ear to wipe them away. "I'm not crying because I'm sad, but because I'm so very happy. Of course I can forgive you."

"Oh, thank you!" squealed Twinkle. Still in the hug, he began jumping up and down, so that the whole group was soon springing about together.

When the hopping finally stopped, Star stepped away from the hug and clapped her golden paws. "So now we can really start the party!"

"Wait a moment, please," Petal said. "I'd like to say something first."

The five bunnies spun on the spot to face Petal. What was she going to say?

"Thank you, Star and Sky, for all you did to fix

things. Thank you, Diamond, for the cake. And thank you, Twinkle and Ruby, for making up. I was worried our friendship was ruined. But now I know we'll be friends for ever. I feel so lucky!" Petal flapped her ears up high with happiness. "And NOW we can start the party!" she declared. She held up a piece of barknote – it was the list Ruby had helped Petal to write.

Activities for my burrow party

Apple bobbing

Six-legged race

Balloon pop

Musical rabbits

Pin the tail on the bunny

The lucky daisy game

Pass the parsnip

Karaoke

Twinkle squeaked with worry when he saw karaoke on the list. "We don't have to do karaoke," he said quickly. "It's Petal's party – she should choose!"

Ruby flicked her curly whiskers to agree with Twinkle. "We shouldn't have been arguing about what to do in the first place," she said. "It's your party, Petal!"

"Can we do them all?" Petal asked. "I know there's a lot on the list, but I really don't want to miss out on anything!"

And so the friends did every single thing. Star won the apple bobbing, and Diamond and Sky were joint winners of the six-legged race. No one really won the balloon pop – although all the balloons got burst! With her excellent hearing, Petal won musical rabbits, and Ruby won pin the tail on the bunny. They each ate so many lucky daisies during the daisy game that no one could work out who won, but Twinkle was the clear winner of pass the parsnip and ended up with a gigantic pile of the vegetables!

They followed the list exactly, ending with karaoke, where they sang and made up funny dances. None of the bunnies could actually sing very well, but no one cared – except perhaps Petal's parents, who were in the room next door and had to stick acorns in their ears.

The six friends were back together, and they felt like the luckiest bunnies in Bright Burrow.

You're in luck!

Read on for a sneak peek at what the hoppiest, floppiest, pluckiest, luckiest bunnies around are getting up to next in *Diamond's Dream!*

ONE
Seeing the Future

Diamond sat down on the soft warm sand of Paradise Beach, as close as she could get to Mirror Lake without getting her fur wet. She leaned forward to look into the water. Diamond's reflection floated back at her, her pink eyes blinking, her white glossy head resting in her little paws.

"Hey, Diamond!" someone called from behind her, making Diamond jump. She turned to see Sky and Star walking towards her. Well, Star was walking, with her golden tail swooshing from side to side. But Sky was cartwheeling, flinging up sand with her fluffy blue paws as she spun around and around.

Diamond smiled at her friends, or at least she tried to. But the corners of her mouth wouldn't stop creeping back down again.

"What are you doing?" Star asked, stopping beside Diamond and looking around at the white-yellow sand. "Are you digging for surprises?"

Paradise Beach was known for magical surprises that were sometimes buried under the sand. Not long ago, Diamond had found a beautiful glow shell that lit up like magic. She kept it on her bedside table at home.

Diamond shook her head but didn't explain what she *was* doing.

"Ooh, I know!" Sky chirruped, clapping her paws together. "You're going for a swim, right?"

"Don't be silly, Sky," Star said before Diamond could reply. "It's far too cold for that."

Diamond nodded. She wasn't so keen on swimming even when it was really warm and sunny. She seemed to splash so much more than her friends did, and worried that it might annoy other bunnies nearby.

"So what *are* you doing then?" Sky kept on, a frown forming across her fluffy blue head. "Is everything OK?"

"I'm fine," Diamond said. "I was just..." She flapped a paw at the lake.

Sky flipped into the air and landed with her back paws in the water. "I've got it! You were trying to read your future! Ooh, I love doing that." Sky peered over the water so far that her little blue nose got wet. "I think I see something... Oh, nope, that's just you, Star."

Star was behind Sky, pulling her back. "Mirror Lake can't really show our futures, you know."

Sky spun around, splashing water everywhere. "Sure it can!" she squeaked. "Last week I saw the biggest, tastiest dandelion cake in the reflection, and the next morning my dad had made one. I didn't even ask for it or anything!"

"Well, I can't see anything anyway," Diamond said quietly.

Star frowned. "What were you hoping to see?" she asked, putting a golden paw to her chin.

Diamond sighed and explained, "I thought the lake might show me what my mum and dad are getting me for my birthday tomorrow."

Sky stared into the water again. "Are you sure you can't see anything at all?" she asked.

Diamond shrugged and looked down again, too. "Not really, just my own reflection. . . I look a bit small though, as if it's showing me in the past, not the future! Definitely no desk for my bedroom. That's what I've been dreaming about for my birthday. I've mentioned it to my mum and dad burrows of times!"

The Owls of Blossom Wood

Katie, Eva and Alex know a secret – when they hide inside a hollow tree trunk at the bottom of Katie's garden, they find themselves whisked away to a magical wood alive with animals, where they're no longer girls but owls!

The Unicorns of Blossom Wood

When cousins Cora, Isabelle and Lei discover magical hoofprints in the ground, they're carried away to an amazing land where they're no longer girls ... they're unicorns!

The Puppies of Blossom Meadow

Erin, Amber and Kayla are best friends who LOVE dogs. So when they discover an enchanted collar that transforms them into adorable puppies and whisks them to the beautiful Blossom Meadow, it's the best day ever!

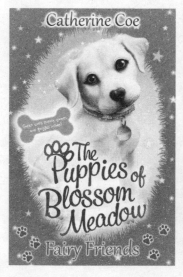